To
dEAR
Evelyn
who is learning to read!

love,
GAGA

MW00916329

Dec
2020

TODAY

Evelyn

WILL BE A

PRINCESS

Andrews McMeel
Publishing®

a division of Andrews McMeel Universal

PRINCESS
Evelyn

[PASTE PHOTO HERE]

FULL NAME: EVELYN BALZK

AGE: 5

Evelyn,

this book is for you!

FROM: _____

MESSAGE: _____

_____

_____

Today,
Evelyn
will be a princess.

She'll get to wear
pretty dresses
that swish
and swirl . . .

and
sparkly shoes
that make her
feel fancy.

Evelyn
will ride in
a royal carriage
wherever
she goes . . .

and wear
the most
beautiful
crown covered
with jewels.

But, mommy
says princesses
don't get
to play in
the mud.

Maybe
Evelyn
will be
a princess
tomorrow . . .

PRINCESS
Evelyn's
FAVORITE THINGS

COLOR:
_____

FOOD:
_____

GAME:
_____

ANIMAL:
_____

SONG:
_____

MOVIE:
_____

Today I'll Be a Princess copyright © 2015 by Andrews McMeel Publishing.
All rights reserved. Printed in the United States of America. No part of this
book may be used or reproduced in any manner whatsoever without written
permission except in the case of reprints in the context of reviews.

Andrews McMeel Publishing
a division of Andrews McMeel Universal
1130 Walnut Street, Kansas City, Missouri 64106

www.andrewsmcmeel.com

Library of Congress Control Number: 2014946447

Written by Paula Croyle
Illustrated by Heather Brown

CPSIA information can be obtained
at www.ICGtesting.com
Printed in the USA
BVHW021050010819
554878BV00014B/371/P